This book belongs to:

_____

Acknowledgements

Firstly, I would love to thank God for His Blessings.

I would also like to thank my daughter, Alyssa for being the best daughter ever, and my husband, James for his continuous love.

A big thank you also goes to my loving mother, Marylene, for being my strength always.

To add, I would like to thank my dad, sisters and brothers for their encouragements, and of course, not to forget my real Jasper, the most adorable dog ever, who inspired me to write these great adventures.

Finally, a huge thank you goes out to: Nadia Ilchuk, for those beautiful and amazing illustrations; Sam Wright, my editor; Istvan Szabo, for formatting all my books, and everyone else who helped to make my dream become a reality.

Other books in Jasper the Island Hopper Series:
1. Jasper the Island Hopper; A Day on Mahé.
2. Jasper the Island Hopper; An Adventure on Praslin.
3. Jasper the Island Hopper; A Trip to La Digue
4. Jasper the Island Hopper; A Boat Ride

For more updates, kindly follow author:
https://www.facebook.com/Audrey-Lavigne-Author-611559249499532/
https://www.amazon.com/AUDREY-LAVIGNE/e/B08KWM8DV3
https://www.audreylavigneauthor.com

Christmas Countdown with

Jasper

The Island Hopper

Book 5 of Jasper the Island Hopper series

AUDREY LAVIGNE

Illustrated by Nadia Ilchuk

Jasper, the island hopper,
Is a small white dog who is very fluffy.
He enjoys island hopping,
But for this holiday, he is too busy.

Jasper is feeling happy and gay.
His favourite day of the year,
Is only seven days away!
YES! Christmas is almost here.

Every year it's the same for Jasper,
He has a long list of things to do,
But he will tackle one activity per day,
For his Christmas to be good.

Christmas
to do list

1. Write a letter to Father Christmas
2. Decorate his Christmas tree
3. Go shopping for Christmas cards
4. Bake a Christmas pudding
5. Buy Christmas gifts for his family and friends
6. Wrap his gifts and write his cards
7. Go to church on Christmas Eve

With seven days away,
From Christmas day,
Jasper grabs a blank paper,
And writes a beautiful letter.

Dear Santa,
Once again,
We have been good,
Not one single day,
Where we have been rude.
We pray that on Christmas day,
You will not forget about us three.
We don't have snow here,
So, you won't see a chimney.
Use the front door to come in.
Love, Jasper, Alyssa, and Benji.

Six days away from Christmas day!
Jasper is going to decorate,
His big Christmas tree today.
He really wants it to look great.

He bought a nice enormous tree,
He is adding colourful garlands to it,
Jasper will feel very happy,
After placing a bright start at its tip.

10

There are five days to go,
Before Jasper hears HO! HO! HO!
He is now at the cards store.
Which ones should he go for?

Jasper has a lot of cards in his hands,
All with amazing pictures and colours.
He needs to buy for all of his friends,
As well as for his adorable owners.

13

Jasper's excitement is increasing,
He has four days left only.
Today, he is baking a Christmas pudding.
He uses a traditional Seychellois recipe.

Jasper starts with sugar and butter,
He whisks them together.
Then he adds raisins, eggs and flour,
For 8 hours, he cooks it in boiling water.

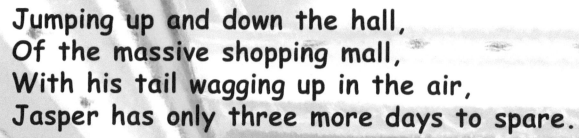

Jumping up and down the hall,
Of the massive shopping mall,
With his tail wagging up in the air,
Jasper has only three more days to spare.

16

Jasper has to buy some nice gifts.
The joy of giving means a lot for him.

17

The excitement is building up!
Do you feel it, too?
Two more days before Christmas.
One….Two…. WOOHOO!

Jasper is busy wrapping the gifts.
A beautiful bracelet for Alyssa,
And a big hard bone for Benji.
He also writes their cards. VOILA!

20

Today it's Christmas Eve.
It's the day before Christmas.
Every year Jasper makes it a must,
To attend the midnight mass.

Christmas is not only a festive holiday,
For the good food and nice gifts.

Jesus was born on this day,
So, it is also his birthday.

Today is the big day.
Christmas is finally here!
Jasper rushes to the Christmas tree.
Sadly, he cannot find a gift,
That has his name on it!

What a sad Christmas for Jasper!

23

Suddenly, Jasper hears a voice.
"HO! HO! HO! Merry Christmas!"
It's Santa Claus!

"I am sorry for being late.
But, better late than never."
Father Christmas says.
"I received your lovely letter.
My gifts will make you feel better."

Jasper opens his gift in a flash,
And couldn't believe his eyes.
A nice hat and a pair of sunglasses,
What a wonderful surprise!

27

Jasper has done it again this year.
He has done everything on his list.
He dances to his favourite song,
'Jingle bells, Jingle bells,
Jingle all the way.'

Both, Alyssa and Benji,
Are also enjoying themselves.
The Christmas pudding is so yummy,
And it has a very Christmassy smell.

"Until next year,
Have a Merry Christmas.
And a Happy New Year.
With love, Jasper,
The island hopper,
From the sunny Seychelles."

30

Hope you enjoyed this beautiful story.

Try and answer these questions.

1. Which day of the year is Jasper's favourite?

2. How many days does Jasper have to prepare for Christmas?

3. Who is Jasper's best buddy and what did he buy him?

4. Who is Jasper's owner and what did he buy her?

5. What did Jasper get from father Christmas?

Well done!

Lightning Source UK Ltd.
Milton Keynes UK
UKHW051846110821
388659UK00002B/11